Return to the Cave of Time

U-VENTURES™

Return to the Cave of Time

EDWARD PACKARD

Illustrated by DREW WILLIS

SIMON & SCHUSTER BOOKS *for* YOUNG READERS

New York London Toronto Sydney New Delhi

SIMON & SCHUSTER BOOKS FOR YOUNG READERS
An imprint of Simon & Schuster Children's Publishing Division
1230 Avenue of the Americas, New York, New York 10020
This book is a work of fiction. Any references to historical events, real people, or real locales are used fictitiously. Other names, characters, places, and incidents are products of the author's imagination, and any resemblance to actual events or locales or persons, living or dead, is entirely coincidental.
Copyright © 1985, 2010 by Edward Packard
CHOOSE YOUR OWN ADVENTURE is a registered trademark of Chooseco LLC, which is not associated in any manner with this product or U-VENTURES, Edward Packard, Simon & Schuster, Inc., or Expanded Apps, Inc.
U-VENTURES is a trademark of Edward Packard.
All rights reserved, including the right of reproduction in whole or in part in any form.
SIMON & SCHUSTER BOOKS FOR YOUNG READERS is a trademark of Simon & Schuster, Inc.
For information about special discounts for bulk purchases, please contact Simon & Schuster Special Sales at 1-866-506-1949 or business@simonandschuster.com.
The Simon & Schuster Speakers Bureau can bring authors to your live event. For more information or to book an event, contact the Simon & Schuster Speakers Bureau at 1-866-248-3049 or visit our website at www.simonspeakers.com.
Book design by Hilary Zarycky
The text for this book is set in ITC Galliard.
The illustrations for this book are rendered in pen and ink.
Manufactured in the United States of America
0212 OFF
10 9 8 7 6 5 4 3 2 1
Library of Congress Cataloging-in-Publication Data
Packard, Edward, 1931–
Return to the Cave of Time / Edward Packard ; illustrated by Drew Willis. — 1st ed.
p. cm. — (U-ventures)
The reader once again enters the mysterious Cave of Time and by following the instructions on each page can have several different adventures backward and forward in time.
ISBN 978-1-4424-3427-1 (pbk. : alk. paper) — ISBN 978-1-4424-5283-1 (eBook)
1. Plot-your-own stories. [1. Time travel—Fiction. 2. Adventure and adventurers—Fiction. 3. Plot-your-own stories.] I. Willis, Drew, ill. II. Title.
PZ7.P1245Re 2012
[Fic]—dc23
2011020270

Humans are great at inventing things, and what we can't invent, we can imagine. For example, we can imagine what it would be like to journey into the future or into the past. You can do it yourself. Just start reading this book.

This is no ordinary book.

Some strange things happen in it, one of which I'd better tell you about.

In your travels you will meet someone who can give you special information, like a secret word. Be sure to remember it.

Now it's time for our story to begin. I mean *your* story. It is just a story, but in some ways it's like life itself: Some of what happens depends on luck, but a lot depends on decisions you make. Try to think clearly. And enjoy your adventures.

Wherever you go, whatever decisions you make, I wish you well.

Edward Packard

Your heart races as you make your way through Snake Canyon, looking for the entrance to the Cave of Time. About midafternoon you reach the familiar grove of pine trees near the cave's entrance, only to find that landslides covered it over.

You are not one to give up easily. You search the floor of the canyon, looking for another way in. It's not until the sun is about to go down that you find one, a hole barely big enough to squeeze through, hidden by clumps of sage. You crawl in on your hands and knees, and then along a tunnel that you hope leads to the main chamber of the cave.

The tunnel seems endless and keeps curving to one side, as if it might be going around in a circle. After a half hour of crawling, your hands and knees are sore. You feel a tightening of muscles in your throat—the beginning of panic. There's not enough room to turn around, and you're not sure you can back out!

The only thing to do is to keep going, so that's what you do, painfully crawling around a bend to the right, then one to the left, in total darkness. Stopping to rest, you hear a voice singing ahead of you, an eerie tune with only three or four notes. You crawl on, and a minute later reach a dimly lit chamber. A thin, ghostlike figure

with a long white beard is singing. Seeing you, he sings a few more notes, then holds up a hand.

As if to answer your question before you ask it, this strange man—if he is a man—says, "You have found the Oracle of Time."

You are amazed to meet anyone in the cave, much less an oracle. You feel a flash of fear, afraid that you are in his power, but as you study his face, you can't help but smile. There is a playful, impish look in his eyes. You wonder if he can tell you some things you've wondered about, so you start asking questions: "If you are the Oracle of Time, can you tell me, what is time?"

The oracle is silent for a moment, then answers in a firm voice: "Time is what keeps everything from happening at once."

You are not sure what he means by that, but you continue: "When did time start? And when will it end?"

"Would you like to see?" he asks.

You gulp in amazement. "Sure."

"What then—the beginning of time, or the end?"

Say "the beginning," turn to page 4.
Say "the end," turn to page 7.

"I'd like to see the beginning," you say. Instantly you find yourself weightless, floating in totally black space! There are no stars or suns or moons or wisps of light; no breath of air; no sound; no smell or taste; no up or down or sideways; no motion; no feeling—nothing but silence.

Suddenly a point of light so brilliant it feels like pins driven into your eyeballs flashes and, sooner than you can blink, expands like a million lightning bolts.

You instinctively shut your eyes, but the light is still painfully bright. You move your hands to cover your eyes. You scream—but no sound comes.

Darkness returns.

Your eyes have adjusted once again to the dim light of the chamber of the oracle. He is still standing where he was. You feel shaken by your experience. You're not eager to try something like that again, but you are still curious about time.

"Tell me," you say, "did anything happen before time began? Could anything happen after time ends?"

"Nothing can happen unless time is passing," the oracle says. "But things could happen in another time frame, *outside* our time. Then another time would be passing."

You think for a moment, then ask, "Could I ever visit another time frame, where another time is passing?"

"It is possible," the oracle replies. "The Cave of Time has passageways that lead to places where you perceive others as they will be in their future, while they perceive you as you were in your past, as well as places where you perceive others as they were in their past, while they perceive you as you will be in your future."

Your head feels clogged with thoughts you can't absorb. "I'd rather stay where everybody is in the same time," you say.

"That may be possible, but possibly it may not," says the oracle. "Which shall it be for you then, the future or the past?"

"Just a minute," you say.

"What's the problem?"

"I want to visit another time, but I'm afraid I might end up in a terrible time and place. It might be in the time of the black plague in medieval Europe, or far in the future when Earth is swallowed up by the sun."

"I suppose so," the oracle says. "But that would be unusual."

"Still, it's something to think about," you say.

The oracle pulls on his long beard. He seems to be thinking, and it's taking him a long time, which is not surprising, for he has all the time in the world!

"All right," he finally says. "I'll give you a secret word. You may only be able to use it once to escape if you don't like the time you're in. The secret word is 'Calypso.' But remember this: You may only be able to use it once! Now let's not waste time. Which shall it be for you, the future or the past?"

Say "the future," turn to page 14.

Say "the past," turn to page 25.

"I'd like to see the end of time," you say, "as long as it isn't the end of me!"

You wonder if the oracle heard the last part, but aren't able to ask because in less time than the blink of an eye you find yourself weightless, floating in silent space. The light of a sun much larger than your own sun shines so brilliantly that you throw your hands up to cover your eyes.

It's not until that moment that you realize you are rolling over and over in space, like meat on a spit. The side of you facing the sun is so hot, it would burst into flame if it weren't cooled as you turn away from the light.

For seconds—or is it minutes or hours?— you rotate like a misshapen asteroid, heating, then cooling, then heating again. All the while the enormous sun is shrinking ever more rapidly, while growing ever more brilliant, until you can see bright light even though you're shielding your eyes. Then darkness surrounds you.

Once again you are in the chamber of the oracle, blinking as your eyes adjust to the dim light.

"The end of time was quite something," you tell the oracle. "Tell me, did anything happen before time began? Could anything happen after time ends?"

"Nothing can happen unless time is passing," the oracle answers. "But things could happen in another time frame, *outside* our time. Then another time would be passing."

You think for a moment, then ask, "Could I ever visit another time frame, where another time is passing?"

"It is possible," the oracle replies. "The Cave of Time has passageways that lead to places where you perceive others as they will be in their future, while they perceive you as you were in your past, as well as places where you perceive others as they were in their past, while they perceive you as you will be in your future."

You try, but you can't be sure what the oracle is saying.

"I think I'd rather stay in my own time frame," you say.

"Very well," says the oracle. "Which shall it be then, the future or the past?"

"Just a minute," you say.

"What's the problem?"

"I want to visit another time, but I'm afraid I might end up in a terrible time and place. It might be in the time of the black plague in medieval Europe, or far in the future when Earth is swallowed up by the sun."

"I suppose so," the oracle says. "But that would be unusual."

"Still, it's something to think about," you say.

The oracle pulls on his long beard. He seems to be thinking, and it's taking him a long time, which is not surprising, for he has all the time in the world!

"All right," he finally says. "I'll give you a secret word you can use to escape if you don't like the time you're in. The secret word is 'Calypso.'"

"Thanks, I feel a little less worried now," you say.

"Good," he says. "But remember this: You may only be able to use it once! Now let's not waste time. Which shall it be for you, the future or the past?"

Say "the future," turn to page 14.
Say "the past," turn to page 25.

You decided to risk crossing to the bus station, but cars, trucks, and buses are coming along all the time. Traffic is very heavy. There's no way you could cross against the light.

Traffic comes to a stop. You have a green light to cross. But you're three minutes ahead of time. It might have been red three minutes ago. If it was, you might not know it until you're hit by a truck.

You stand on the corner, timing the traffic lights. They change between red and green every forty-five seconds. There, they just turned green. Normally, that would mean you could cross. But you're wondering whether that still holds. Let's see, you think, if they just turned green, they must have just turned red forty-five seconds ago. You keep working back to three minutes ago, when the drivers of trucks think the light is changing just as you do, but are they thinking it's changing to red or to green?

Now it's been green awhile. You're feeling a little dizzy. Maybe it was red three minutes ago. You run the numbers again through your head. No, you're sure it was green three minutes ago.

Or was it red? Now it's turned red again. The cars and trucks are whizzing by. Your head aches, but you can't just do nothing. The light is still red, but it will turn green soon.

Go when it turns green, continue to page 13.
Wait till it turns red again, turn to page 73.

The light for crossing turns green. The cars and trucks stop at the intersection. You feel sure they just stopped three minutes ago too. You run across the street . . . and make it!

You reach the terminal and board the bus to Denver.

From there you'll have to switch buses a couple of times to reach the village nearest to Snake Canyon.

You are on the road for three days, scavenging food wherever you can, traveling by bus and on foot. At last, you find Snake Canyon and, after trekking most of the day, reach the entrance to the Cave of Time. It's scary going back in, but there is no doubt in your mind that it's what you have to do. Living three minutes ahead of your own time would condemn you to a life of hopeless confusion.

You walk through the entrance and take small steps ahead, but your eyes haven't adjusted to the dim light. You trip and fall. Suddenly you're sliding down a chute, headed for another time. . . .

Turn to page 57.

You are lying in an open silk-lined box. Is it a coffin? Not exactly. You are hooked up to a tube and wires, as if you were in a hospital. Yet you don't feel sick. You feel well—very well in fact, though you can't sit up.

Something you can't see is holding you down. You hear soothing, almost hypnotic, chords of music. The light in the room shifts from sky blue to yellow green to red orange to blue again. Moving your hand to your scalp, you feel wires coming out of your head.

Where are you? How did you get here? Suddenly you remember—you traveled through the Cave of Time, and you asked to see the future. This situation is so weird that you must be *far* in the future.

Looking around, you see that you are in a long narrow space that reminds you of the cabin of an airliner. On either side of you, other coffins—you can't think of a better word for them—extend as far as you can see in both directions. The ceiling is invisible because of a dense fog that hovers a few feet over your head. It's as if you were in the middle of a weird dream; yet you don't feel scared. Even though you're held prisoner, you feel pleasurable sensations, as if you were eating your favorite ice cream while hearing great music, while seeing a beautiful sunset. Whoever has captured you must have hooked a wire into the pleasure center of your brain!

The music changes key. A robotic arm places a clear plastic mask over your mouth. You start to gasp for breath, but then realize you don't need to—oxygen is being fed into the mask. A moment later your coffin tilts, sliding you into a tank of warm water that's moving rapidly, as if it were a swiftly flowing stream.

Instinctively you start swimming against the current. Thanks to your oxygen mask you have no problem breathing. You stroke and kick hard, glad to be exercising your muscles and relieving the tension of being confined in a box. Your tubes and wires are still firmly in place, and your body is held in straps under your shoulders and around your waist.

This must be how people keep their muscles from wasting away, you think. Ingenious but horrible. Everything is decided for you. You go through the motions, but you have no choices. The people who rule this world must think they are providing the perfect life, but it's more like a perfect prison!

Suddenly the current is flowing more swiftly. As you speed up your strokes, you feel even more pleasurable sensations. You swim faster, faster, until even with almost pure oxygen flowing into your mask, you're reaching the limit of endurance. Then, as if some computer has been monitoring you and knows that you can't swim any harder, the current eases.

The water level falls, and you are left weightless, suspended in warm air currents that blow and swirl about your body. In less than a minute you are dry. Robotic arms lift you back into your coffin. Your life—if you can call it that—goes on as before.

You have been lying quietly, trying to adjust to the reality that lies ahead, when you are startled to hear a voice. It must be entering your brain through one of the implanted wires. It speaks in clear but stilted English.

"You have been identified as an alien intruder. Your bioanalysis shows an 87.37 percent probability that you can understand the English language. Based on your brain-wave reaction to the preceding statement, the probability that you understand the English language has increased to 99.97 percent. Stand by for transport."

A moment later you lose consciousness.

Turn to page 18.

You're awake again, seated in a chair. Whenever you move, the chair adjusts itself so that it's molded to your body, giving you the most perfect and comfortable support imaginable.

A woman is seated near you. Her body and face seem elongated, as if she were an image in an amusement park mirror; yet her face is beautiful, and her olive-hued eyes are warm.

"You are an alien of uncertain origin," she says gently. "Our computer will determine what can be done for you."

"Who are you?" you ask. "And where am I?"

"My name is Celeste Four-Three-Three. I am your overseer. You are on Colony Suprema Eighty-Seven to the Fifth Power, Proxima Neptuna, Galactica Virgo Eight Hundred and Four, and you are very fortunate to be here. Through advanced technology all problems of life have been solved, all needs taken care of. There is nothing for our people to do but to exist in a state of perpetual pleasure."

A sharply focused light beams at your face, increases in brightness for a moment, and then fades. Celeste 433 continues, "Our monitors show that you are not completely happy in the supremely pleasurable life we have made possible for you. You must have an irrational quality in your personality, obviously acquired in your previous culture. This could cause difficulty. Therefore, I must ask you: Will you accept your good fortune and a life of perpetual pleasure, or will your thoughts and actions become rebellious? Answer truthfully. Our monitors will show if you lie."

Say you'll accept a life of perpetual pleasure,
turn to page 23.

Say you cannot accept such a life, turn to page 34.

You're worried that you could be hit by a car whose driver won't be able to see you for three minutes. You don't dare cross any streets, and if you can't cross any streets, you're stuck at this school—three minutes ahead of your own time!

At least this way you won't get killed. You walk aimlessly back into the school building, sit on the bench outside the principal's office, and bury your face in your hands, trying to think of what to do.

You've been sitting there for three minutes when someone taps your shoulder.

"I didn't see you sit down. Is anything wrong?"

You look up and see the kindly face of Ms. Rangos, who works in the school office. "I don't know—I'm three minutes ahead of my own time," you say.

"Please look up and talk to me," Ms. Rangos says. "I want to help you."

"I *am* talking," you start to say, but then you realize that Ms. Rangos won't hear those words for three minutes more. She must think you're just sitting there silently. The only reason she can see you is that you've been sitting in the same position for more than three minutes.

There is nothing you can do except explain everything as well as you can and hope that someone will be standing there three minutes from now and will hear what you said three minutes earlier.

Ms. Rangos goes off and returns with the school nurse and the principal. They are all standing there three minutes after you explained your situation. Now you're just sitting there, but they hear you explaining what happened in the Cave of Time. They don't believe it, of course, and decide that you must be sick. They take you to the hospital, where the doctors give you a sedative, and you fall asleep.

When you wake up, several doctors are standing by your bed, talking to one another. Next to them is a blackboard on which these words are written:

> We could tell from your brain patterns that you are several minutes ahead of us. When you wake up and read this, we won't know it because you are living ahead of our time. It's for this reason that we aren't talking to you. Erase this and write your own message. We'll be able to read it in a few

minutes. We don't know any cure for your strange condition, but we will do our best to help you.

You read the message twice, feeling grateful that you are safe and that people understand what the problem is. What will you write on the blackboard? What will life be like if you are always three minutes ahead of everyone else? You think a moment, then write:

I'D JUST LIKE TO GO HOME. I GUESS I'D BETTER TAKE THIS BLACKBOARD WITH ME.

Three minutes later the doctors smile as they see you writing on the blackboard. They give you the blackboard to take with you, as well as a recorder, and instructions to hand out so people will understand how to behave toward you.

No doubt about it, life is going to be complicated living three minutes ahead of everyone else. Maybe you can make money betting on horse races!

The End

You decide that pleasure is what everyone spends their life seeking. If you're lucky enough to have it handed to you, you might as well take it.

"I'll accept a life of pleasure," you say.

Even as you speak, you feel yourself passing out.

You are awake again, after how long you have no idea. Once again you're in your "coffin." You lie back and try to enjoy the pleasurable sensations you're feeling and not think of anything disturbing. This works for a while, but soon you become restless. You are definitely not happy. You try to adjust, to get used to it. What else can you do?

Deep down, you know you made an awful choice.

The days go by. You *think* they go by. You have to guess when one ends and another begins.

Conditions get worse. Pleasure inputs decline. Swimming periods are cut out. Once again you hear a voice:

"Suprema Eighty-Seven to the Fifth Power has been attacked. Our resources must be used to fight the war. The

burden must be shared by everyone. We
will prevail even if we die."

You shudder at this announcement. What
does it mean? You try to remember the secret
word the Oracle of Time gave you. Maybe you
should use it now!

You try to use the secret word.

Say "Calypso," turn to page 45.
Say "nimrod," turn to page 33.

You are in a cave, close to the entrance. For a minute it feels as if your mind has become detached from your body—the feeling of being transported through time. Looking out, you can see that you are high on a mountainside. A vast landscape of plains and lakes and patches of forest stretches beneath you. There is no sign of human habitation. You wonder if you are living thousands of years in the past, perhaps before the appearance of human beings. In the distance you notice dark, moving specks, what might be a herd of grazing animals. Where there's life, there's food, and hope for survival, you think.

You sense a presence nearby. You whirl around, and your eyes meet other eyes. They belong to a boy who looks older than you, though he is a bit shorter. His wavy brown hair is shoulder length. He is naked except for crudely fashioned shorts made of animal skin. He looks more solidly built than any boy you remember. His muscles bulge, as if he has been weight lifting. His bushy eyebrows are set on bony ridges above his eyes, giving him a brutish look, yet there's something sweet and friendly in his expression.

"Hello," you say.

"Iaark," the boy replies.

He steps close and stares at you. At that moment you hear a deep-throated growl. In the dim light near the back of the cave, you can make out an animal of monstrous proportions— a gigantic cave bear, larger than any bear in your own time! Terrified, you stand watching.

The boy edges closer.

He touches you.

"Narga," he says, and pulls at your arm, then starts climbing the sheer wall of the cave, gaining handholds on rough niches in the rock. You watch with amazement as he pulls himself up by his arms alone. A moment later he slips into a cleft in the rock, safely out of reach of the bear. The bear follows the boy with his eyes, then turns toward you and growls so loudly, it shakes your bones. You'd better do something fast!

Try to follow Iaark up the wall of the cave,
turn to page 118.
Run out of the cave, turn to page 116.

"I'll join the mutiny," you say.

"Very well," says Christian. "Then stand clear. There may be the swinging of cutlasses before the morning is over!"

Two seamen lead Captain Bligh to the rail. A third holds a knife to his throat. Other seamen finish lowering the longboat. One of the officers loyal to Captain Bligh lunges at Christian, but the new master of the *Bounty* stops him with an upraised dagger.

After that, Bligh's men climb quickly into the boat. Bligh himself stands at the top of the ladder. A hush falls over the mutinous crew as their former captain searches out each man's eyes with his own. In a firm hoarse voice he says, "I may survive and I may not, but it is certain that every one of you will hang."

The crew is silent. Bligh turns and climbs down into the boat. The lines are cast off. The boat moves away as its occupants pull on their long, heavy oars, setting out on what seems like an impossible search for land.

The *Bounty* swings around, the sails billowing out before the following breeze. The seamen pull on the running ropes, trimming the sails as the ship sets a new course. Fletcher Christian puts you to work chipping rust off the anchor chain. While you work, you have a chance to talk to a friendly seaman.

"We're bound for Tahiti," he says in reply to your question. "We'll be taking on supplies, but we can't stay long. If Captain Bligh makes it to land, the whole British Navy will be looking for us." He draws the edge of his hand across your throat to emphasize his point.

"Then where will Christian take us?" you ask.

The seaman stands up, stretches, and looks toward the horizon. "He's mentioned an island—Pitcairn, it's called. Big and fertile enough to sustain us. The reason no one lives on it is that the entire coast is rockbound—there's no safe place to anchor a ship."

As you consider these facts, you're wishing you were somewhere else. All the same, you're glad not to be in the longboat with Captain Bligh.

Continue to page 29.

A few days later the *Bounty* reaches Tahiti. You marvel at the green mountains jutting out of the sea and the long arc of white sandy beach fringed with coconut trees. A fleet of tiny boats is coming toward the ship.

You stand transfixed at the rail, watching the boats and the Tahitians in them, with their smiling faces and up-reached hands.

Fletcher Christian claps his hand on your shoulder.

"Lock this stowaway in my old cabin," he orders one of the men.

"Why would you do this?" you cry. "I thought I would be treated as well as the others."

"Maybe you will be, but I don't want you ashore. I don't trust you to keep quiet about what happened."

A sailor leads you by the arm and locks you in the first mate's cabin. Through the porthole you can see the beautiful island and smell the scent of jasmine wafting across the water. The porthole is too small for the average person to climb through, but you're pretty sure you could squeeze through.

If you wait until nighttime, you could climb through unnoticed and dive overboard. The ship is anchored only a few hundred yards offshore.

You're sure you could swim that far. On the other hand, you don't know how strong the currents are. And you can't be sure a shark wouldn't get you!

Wiggle through the porthole and try to swim to shore, turn to page 112.

Stay on the ship, turn to page 38.

You climb down a rope into the longboat with Captain Bligh and the men who stayed loyal to him.

From this crowded, bobbing craft, you watch the *Bounty* sail away in the brisk west wind. Soon it is just a speck on the horizon, then it is gone.

Meanwhile, in your boat, four men pull listlessly on the oars while the others slouch against the gunnel. Captain Bligh, grim-faced and motionless, sits in the stern, his hand on a great wooden tiller, moving it from time to time to keep the boat on course through the seething waves. He stares fixedly ahead, as if at any moment he might see land on the horizon.

You know as well as anyone else, for Captain Bligh has said it, that the nearest charted island is more than a thousand miles away, and having no navigational instruments, a small boat could easily miss it.

By midafternoon you feel like a burned potato, and you're thankful when the blazing sun goes behind a cloud. You're terribly thirsty, but Captain Bligh will allow not a drop of water until "six bells," by which he means seven o'clock.

"Drink water during the day," he says, "and you'll just sweat it off."

You slump down on the seat and slip into a trance—half sleeping, half daydreaming, trying to make time pass.

So it goes, day after day after day, through calm and rough seas, under scorching sun and drenching rain. You feel yourself shriveling from lack of food. After three weeks you feel like a dried-up peach.

Day after day after day, no rain falls. The boat's store of water is gone. If rain doesn't come soon, you'll all die of thirst. The men who are supposed to be rowing can barely lift their oars. Captain Bligh sits in the stern, still trying to steer, but he looks as if he can barely keep awake.

You try to remember the secret word the Oracle of Time gave you. But you're too weak and exhausted to think what it is!

You grow steadily weaker and lie sick and feverish in the bilge.

One morning Captain Bligh can't rouse you. One of the officers tries but fails to find your pulse. A few minutes later the men bow their heads while Bligh says some kind words and recites the Lord's Prayer, and they gently lower your body over the side.

The End

You say "nimrod," but nothing happens.

The pleasurable sensations you were experiencing continue to decline. Soon they stop completely. You strain to get out of your coffin, but every time you try, you fall back. Your captors have cut your nutrients and exercise so much that you no longer have the strength to sit up!

Your condition worsens. You feel constant hunger. The lights get dimmer. The music ends. You grow weaker. You're sure that Suprema Eighty-Seven to the Fifth Power is losing the war. You're right. Your coffin is your final resting place.

The End

You tell Celeste 433 that you are not willing to give up your freedom for a life of pleasure. She nods and, to your surprise, smiles. "I understand," she says. "You are from a primitive culture, so you don't understand that constant pleasure is superior to freedom of choice. Very well. Since freedom is more important to you than pleasure, I shall tell you something that I would not have mentioned otherwise. Suprema Eighty-Seven to the Fifth Power may soon be involved in a war between the grand overseers."

"Who are they?"

Celeste 433 dismisses your question with a wave of her long, bony hand.

"Listen. I admire your courage and therefore will give you a chance to survive this war, which I fear will destroy this colony. I shall provide you with a spacecraft, but your troubles will not be over. Space is a vast and hostile wilderness. I know of only two places you can reach where you'll have hope of survival. One of them is Alpha Alpha, a colony beyond Pluto that is far more advanced than this one. In fact, it may be the most advanced in the galaxy. The other place where you might possibly survive is the planet Earth."

"Earth? That's my home planet—I'd really like to get back there."

Celeste 433 shakes her head. "You don't understand. You have been time-displaced. Earth is no longer what it was. It is a scarred and ruined planet, a backward child of the galaxy, an archae-ological scrap heap. I've told you the truth. The decision is yours."

You long to see Earth again, even though it's changed for the worse. You're curious about Alpha Alpha, too, though what you've seen so far of advanced civilizations doesn't encourage you.

Take the spacecraft to Alpha Alpha, turn to page 36.
Take the spacecraft to Earth, turn to page 100.

"I'll go to Alpha Alpha," you say.

"Farewell then," says Celeste 433. "And . . ."

You miss the last part of what she says. Perhaps you lost consciousness. The next thing you know you are aboard a spacecraft, seated in a chair molded to fit your body.

Through the windows you see endless numbers of stars and galaxies.

You have been traveling through space for some time when you notice a luminous cloud ahead. It looks like millions of sparkling drops of water suspended in space. As you approach it, you realize that it's not a cloud at all, but a planet dotted with thousands of lakes. Could this be Alpha Alpha?

You look around your spacecraft. There are a few levers and dials. You try to move a lever, then another, and soon find that the controls are locked. Your flight has been preprogrammed. There's nothing to do but watch, and hope.

You continue to close in on the planet. Little flashes of light are jumping from one region to another. One flash comes right at you. Perhaps the inhabitants have sensed your presence. Being so advanced, they should have no trouble bringing you in for a landing.

To your surprise, your spacecraft veers away from what seemed to be your destination. You watch the planet slip to the side. Ahead now are only a few distant stars.

What's happening? Why didn't you land on Alpha Alpha? You try to hold back your tears, try to think of a reason to have hope. Then you do think of a reason: Celeste 433 said that Alpha Alpha may be the most advanced civilization in the galaxy. Surely such an advanced civilization must be based on love, not cruelty! It must be through love that they have lengthened your journey. Surely there is a good reason for it. Maybe the planet you passed wasn't your destination. Maybe Alpha Alpha lies ahead.

On and on you travel, wondering if you'll get there.

The End

You decide to wait in the first mate's cabin rather than risk escaping and swimming to shore. Even if sharks didn't get you, currents might have carried you out to sea.

A crew member brings you food and water every morning for several days. One morning you hear sounds of the men setting sail, the anchor coming up. A cheer rings out. The *Bounty* is underway!

A key turns in the cabin door, and Fletcher Christian himself looks in. You shrink back from this wild-eyed man who took the *Bounty* from her captain, but Christian smiles broadly. He's in a good mood.

"You're free to walk about the ship," he says. "I've been a bit harsh locking you up. Now that there's no danger of your escaping, you're one of us—the youngest, as it happens. One day you may be the chief of Pitcairn Island."

"That's where we're headed?"

"With a fair wind and a little luck we'll be there in a fortnight."

You rush up the ladder and step out onto the main deck. You look up at the sails billowing before the following wind and at the broad blue sea flecked with whitecaps. With a start you notice several Tahitian women sitting on the afterdeck. Fletcher Christian and some of the other mutineers found wives on Tahiti—women who would join them in starting new families.

As the days pass you learn many of the skills required on a full-rigged ship. But when at last the lonely rockbound island looms ahead, you learn that your new skills mean nothing. Christian tells you that the ship must be wrecked on the coral shoals and sunk lest it attract attention. Soon you will have to learn to gather food and be a primitive farmer on a primitive island, thousands of miles from the mainland. It's not the kind of life you want!

You try to remember the secret word the Oracle of Time gave you. You'd better use it now!

Say "Pequod," turn to page 125.
Say "Calypso," turn to page 49.

The tribe sets out on their migration in the morning. You go with them a short distance, then slip away and set out on your own, following animal trails along the river. You know that modern humans lived in the same region and at the same time as the Neanderthals. With a little luck, you'll find one of their settlements along this river.

Unfortunately, you didn't consider that the population of humans in the world now is only a tiny fraction of what it will be in the twenty-first century. Even in a temperate region, where in your own time you would come upon a town or a city every few miles, here in this time, tens of thousands of years earlier, you can walk for hundreds of miles without seeing a sign of human life.

This is what's happening to you, and now, as the sun sinks lower in the sky, a blustery wind blows in, and heavy dark clouds form to the west. Tonight will be colder than any night before. You're cold and hungry and haven't been able to find shelter. You may not be able to keep your body temperature high enough to last through the night.

Continue to page 41.

You look at the sky and see just a fragment of a rainbow over a high rocky ridge to the east. You feel too tired to climb to the top of the ridge. You'd be lucky to make it before it gets dark, and it's bound to be even windier up there. It would make more sense to go down the slope and spend the night sheltered by thick bushes.

Still, the rainbow is so beautiful, you want to walk toward it.

Climb up the hill toward the rainbow, turn to page 86.
Find shelter for the night in the bushes, turn to page 44.

The sailors set up a long wooden board so it juts several feet over the side of the ship. They push you toward it. You can see the captain on the afterdeck. Apparently, he has decided to let the crew do with you what they will.

As the men push you out onto the plank, you yell at them, "Those people on the lower deck don't deserve this. They are human just like you. If anything, they are better than you!"

The biggest sailor rams you with a mop handle.

"Enough of you!" Others push at you with oars, forcing you to the end of the plank. A second later you tumble into the sea.

There was no way you could rewrite history. At least you were brave enough to demand justice.

The End

You head down the slope and reach an area shielded by thick juniper bushes. You gather fallen leaves and try to make a bed for yourself. Now you have some protection from the wind, but you feel colder than ever.

A cold hard rain begins to fall. You become steadily more chilled. In the next hours the rain turns to sleet, then to snow. By morning you're frozen stiff, food for the vultures when, too late, the sun begins to warm you.

The End

The secret word worked! You know that because you are no longer where you were (or when you were!). You're at the entrance to a dark tunnel. You have a feeling that it leads to the Cave of Time.

Turn to page 48.

You're determined to find your way back to the Cave of Time. You walk along the river, looking for landmarks you remember. Eventually you reach the bottom of a slope that extends down from a mountain—it looks familiar. You climb up the slope, winding around the boulders, stopping from time to time to rest and look around.

You catch yourself sniffing the air as if you were an animal. You wish you had as keen a sense of smell as an animal, but you don't. On the other hand, your eyes are as good as those of most animals, and better than most.

You look around and listen. You can't hear anything. Then you realize that you're stalling, afraid to climb higher. You don't like to admit it, but you're afraid to face the cave bear. It's a danger all right, but sometimes you have to face danger, take risks. You force yourself to be brave, to move on, and you start climbing again.

You have been traveling south. It should be getting warmer, but you haven't gone far enough yet, and now, as you climb, you feel a cold wind coming up.

Again you feel the urge to turn back, and again you make yourself keep going.

You climb only a short distance more. Then you spot it—the entrance to a tunnel—under a great rock outcropping. You would have missed it if you had been walking a few hundred feet to the right or left.

Turn to page 48.

It's risky entering a tunnel when you can't be sure where it leads, but you're not going to turn back now. You have to stoop so low, it would almost be easier to get on your hands and knees, and crawl.

You step on a smooth stone surface. This, too, seems familiar. Another step. The angle pitches forward, then you're sliding, too fast to stop yourself, falling into blackness.

Turn to page 50.

You're in an almost pitch-black tunnel. It seems familiar. You take a step forward, then another. And another. The angle pitches forward. Then you're sliding, too fast to stop yourself, falling into blackness.

Turn to page 57.

You're standing in a smelly, mostly darkened space and feel sure that you're in a different time. Your eyes begin to get used to the dim light. You can now see that you are in a dank room amid a pile of heavy ropes and chains. In one direction the room is narrower than in the other. The floor, ceiling, and walls are made of wood planks. You feel motion under your feet. The whole room seems to be moving up and down and from side to side. An oil lamp, making more smoke than light, swings from the ceiling. You realize that you must be aboard a ship.

A big imposing man in a pale blue shirt appears before you. His half-grown beard only partly covers a long scar across his cheek.

"Oh ho, a stowaway!" he says with a grin, exposing a mouthful of yellow teeth. "You must be a clever one to stay hidden for so long. Well, come with me. We'll see what Fletcher Christian thinks of you."

You follow the man up a ladder and take a welcome breath of fresh air. You're on a ship all right—a sailing ship. By the crudeness of the sails and gear, the old-fashioned rig, and the black iron cannon mounted on deck, you can tell that the time must be hundreds of years in the past.

Your eyes fasten on a long boat mounted on deck. On its stern is painted the name *Bounty*. You realize that you are on the ship famous for a mutiny that occurred in 1789, when most of the crew joined the first mate, Fletcher Christian, in taking over the ship. The mutineers, you remember, put Captain Bligh and those loyal to him into a small, open boat, called a longboat. Their only hope of survival lay in rowing more than a thousand miles to the nearest inhabited island.

As the seaman leads you aft, you notice that two of the ship's officers are bound to one of the masts. A tall, shirtless man is standing near the helmsman, talking heatedly to a group of sailors. He hands them each a knife and a cutlass. So this is the notorious Fletcher Christian!

With a shock you realize the mutiny has already begun!

"Ready then, lads," Christian says to the others. "But mind you, there will be no bloodshed if we can avoid it." Turning to another man, he says, "Stiles, lower the boat!"

As Fletcher Christian is barking out orders, the seaman leads you to him.

"A stowaway, sir," he says loudly.

"Oh ho!" says Christian, staring at you with piercing blue eyes.

You start to explain that you didn't mean to be a stowaway, but you find yourself tongue-tied. Who would believe that you got on the *Bounty* through the Cave of Time? Christian looks at you with a quizzical but friendly expression.

"I admire your spirit," he says. "So, instead of throwing you overboard, which is what you deserve, I'll give you a choice. You can join us in taking over the ship, or go with Captain Bligh in the longboat."

You look over at Captain Bligh. Two men have him, one by each arm. He spits at one of them, who, in return, gives him a sharp blow on his forehead, drawing blood.

"Make your decision," Christian says to you, "or we'll toss you to the sharks."

"Stay with Fletcher Christian," shouts Captain Bligh, "and you'll follow him straight to the gallows!"

Join the mutineers and risk hanging, turn to page 27.

Join Captain Bligh and risk starving or drowning, turn to page 31.

You are angry—angry for the people around you and at those who assigned them to this fate. You try desperately to free them. The clanging chains are heard on deck.

"What are you people up to now?" a man shouts into the dark crevices of the hold. "Keep still, or you'll get no water tonight!"

Without thinking, you climb the ladder to the hatch above.

"Let these people free!" you shout.

A sailor opens the hatch and motions for you to come out. "Who are you?" he demands, slamming the hatch shut behind you.

"Can't you see they're hurting?" you yell. "Let them go!"

In the next moment the hatch opens again. The man grips your arm and presses a dagger against your throat. The blade cuts your skin. You feel yourself growing faint. You pass out.

When you come to, you are lying on the top deck with at least ten sailors staring at you. The man you first encountered pulls you to your feet and shakes you.

"I don't know where you came from," he says, "or why you aren't chained like the rest, but you won't be living long!"

"Do you think you can start a rebellion on this ship without being punished?" yells a red-faced man.

"Here's what we do with scum like you," says another, tugging at your clothes. "We make them walk the plank."

You try to remember the secret word the Oracle of Time gave you. You need to use it now!

Say "bolero," turn to page 43.
Say "Calypso," turn to page 56.

The secret word worked!

You know that because you are back in your own time, reading this book, and you've just gotten to . . .

The End

Somewhere a voice is singing. As your eyes slowly adjust to the pale green light, you realize that you are once again in the chamber of the Oracle of Time. The thin, ghostlike figure you remember stops singing. He looks at you intently.

You can hardly find words, but, as if to answer your question before you ask it, this strange man—if he is a man—says, "You have found the Oracle of Time."

"Don't you remember? We've met before," you say. "I must be going around in circles. Can you help me get back to my own time?"

"Sometimes time goes around in circles," the oracle says. "Some break out of the circle; some don't."

"How can I break out?"

"This, my child, is something you must learn for yourself."

"All right," you say doubtfully.

You are about to ask another question when he says, "To begin, you must go to the future or the past. Which do you say it shall be?"

To the future, turn to page 14.
To the past, turn to page 25.

You watch while, like some robotic garbage collector, the spider vehicle lifts your spacecraft off the ground and ascends into the clouds, leaving you standing helplessly on the barren, rust-colored ground. A loneliness sweeps over you worse than any you experienced in space. You strap on your backpack and start walking over the flat, rubble-strewn terrain, trying to travel in a straight line.

The sun never shows through the clouds; the sky gets darker. Nightfall will soon be upon you. You have no idea how far you've traveled or how far you are from civilization—if there is any civilization in this sad world.

Soon it's almost completely dark. At least you're not cold. You lie on the hard, sandy ground and try to sleep. You manage to doze off.

You're awakened abruptly by a sound overhead. Opening your eyes, you see the spider vehicle hovering above you. The wires are already unreeling. You jump up, yelling at the craft above, hoping someone onboard will hear you, but no one answers. Instead, wires drop down and get in position to wrap around you.

You realize that this craft must be manned by

a robot that can't distinguish living beings from stray objects. You feel the wires, like great snakes, holding you fast while the vehicle ascends, carrying out its programmed instructions to take loose objects like you to the landfill.

The End

You turn abruptly and make your way back to the riverbank. Vor yells something after you. You don't understand what he's saying, but you know it isn't friendly. The others, still trying to pick their way across the river, don't notice what happened.

You wade out of the water and follow the trail back to the camp, anxious to get there before dark. You have grown tougher and leaner living with the Neanderthals and make good time.

After a couple of hours you recognize a place you passed before—two fallen pines whose trunks lie across each other, forming a large *X*. You sit on the mossy ground to rest, sure that you haven't far to go.

As your muscles relax, you let your eyes roam over the thickly laced canopy above. What an enormous variety of trees and vines exist in this age! The sky is a more intense blue than you have ever seen. The bark on the trees, the insects hovering, and a bird perched on a limb are all so sharply defined that they seem super real.

Your thoughts are broken by the scream of a raven—danger! You whirl in time to see an enormous snake coiled to strike, its copper-colored head a foot from your knee. You jump sideways, then sprint to get well clear of it.

Continuing at a slower pace, you reflect on the price to be paid for living in a beautiful, unspoiled world: You must be ever alert for danger.

The terrain ahead looks familiar. The Neanderthal campsite is close by. You call out, "Azog, Larga, Mi!"

No answer comes back. You soon see why. The camp is empty, stripped. You run to the river. The raft is gone. They must have finished gathering supplies and started down the river. Now you are alone, and as far as you know, there is no other tribe in the region.

You don't have the strength or time to make a raft of your own. The days are getting cooler, and the nights are already cold. The first snow of the winter could come at any time. Game is abundant, but you are not an experienced hunter. You don't know how to start a fire without matches. You sit on a rock, trying to think of a plan.

Walk south in hopes of reaching a warmer climate and finding a friendly tribe, turn to page 126.

Try to make it through the winter at the present camp, waiting for the Neanderthals to return in the spring, turn to page 74.

Try to get back to the Cave of Time, turn to page 46.

"Let me out!" you yell as you knock on the hatch leading to the deck above. Before you can yell again, an older sailor with a red bandanna pulls up the hatch.

"Where did you come from?" he yells in your face.

Before you can say anything he drags you up onto the deck, into the dazzling sunlight. He pushes you toward some sailors who are sitting on the deck playing cards.

"Look what we have here! A stowaway," he says with a chuckle. "Must have slipped on at our last port in Africa."

Laughing, the sailors begin to push you from one to another.

"Don't hurt me!" you say. "I have no family or home. I want to start a new life in the New World—in America."

"Let me tell you what we do with stowaways," jeers the man you first encountered.

"Please!" you scream.

Just then an older, well-groomed man walks toward you.

"Don't you men have better things to do?" he says to the sailors. "Back to work with you, or you'll have no rum tonight!"

Grumbling, the seamen disperse.

"I am Captain Montague Ward, the master of this ship," says the man as he pulls you to your feet. "And who are you?"

You repeat your story about being an orphan. Captain Ward leads you to his quarters and gives you food and drink.

"You were foolish to stow away on a ship like this," he says. "These men have little regard for human life."

"I might think the same of you, sir," you say, "judging by what I saw belowdecks."

The captain flushes with anger, but you must have touched the right nerve, because the anger quickly leaves his face.

"The truth is, my young friend, I don't know what I'm like anymore. Years ago I got into this business by chance. I needed the money—"

"That's no excuse," you say. "Don't you understand that black people are no different from white people?"

"But of course they are!" the captain snaps. "They are more like animals and—"

"You're ignorant to think so," you interrupt. "Have you been down to the lower deck?"

"Yes, of course," says the captain.

"How can you justify treating them this way? Have you looked at their faces?"

"You don't understand. You are too young. One day—"

"I'll never understand such shameless hypocrisy, such baseness—"

"That's enough!" the captain says sharply. "I should put you in irons for that. But . . . I admire your grit. I'll let you work by washing dishes and cleaning the galley. Who knows? You might amount to something someday."

A week later the ship arrives in Boston. By now you've learned that it's the year 1766. This is the time you'll be living in from now on, trying to get on with your life.

As you watch the crew leading the slaves off the ship, you see Captain Ward standing on the quarterdeck. He notices you and comes over.

"Good luck to you," he says. "This is my last trip on a slave ship, you can be sure."

In that moment, as you look into his eyes, you are content. You haven't changed history, but you're sure that at least one man can lie to himself no more.

The End

"You are brave," Yamara says. "I will accompany you to the cave."

A saucer craft speeds the two of you to a desolate plain on the reshaped American continent. You and Yamara step out of the robot-operated car. The sky seems to be darkening even more than usual. A light drizzle is falling. It feels greasy—you wouldn't want to drink it.

"Rain!" Yamara cries jubilantly. "The cycle of renewal is happening."

"I would think you'd rather have sunshine, since it's always cloudy," you say.

"We must have much rain before the clouds break open," says Yamara. "Then we shall see the sun and sky."

"I wish you could see the Earth the way it was in the twenty-first century," you say.

Ahead of you is a mound with an opening— the entrance to the cave. It doesn't look like anything you remember.

"This is it," says Yamara. "So now it's time to say good-bye. Good luck, if that is possible."

You don't say anything for the moment.

Yamara says, "I can tell that you are worried about what will happen to you."

"It's true," you say. "I'm thinking about how

I could come out of the cave at a really bad time."

"I understand," Yamara says. "I would feel the same way. I wish you the best possible luck."

"Well, thank you," you say. "Good-bye, Yamara."

Yamara returns to his saucer craft. A panel slides shut behind him. You watch as his craft lifts silently off the ground and soars over the desolate landscape.

Alone now, you peer into the entrance of the cave. It's little more than a narrow tunnel leading at an angle into the ground. A damp breeze is blowing out of it.

You shake your head. You're not sure that this is the Cave of Time, but your mind is made up. You take a last look at the barren terrain around you and, hunching over so as not to bump your head, walk slowly into the tunnel.

You have gone only fifty feet or so when the slope steepens, taking you by surprise. You're falling.

Continue to page 67.

You black out—for how long you don't know. Then you can't believe it—it seems impossible—but you are inside your school, standing outside the door to your classroom! Looking in, you see your classmates. Your seat is empty. The teacher, Ms. Hawkins, is talking about the government, explaining what the Supreme Court does.

You've gotten back to your own time! This is better luck than you ever expected. You can just go in and take your seat, but how will you explain why you've been away from school?

You're tempted to keep out of sight, but you realize that you'll have to explain eventually. Glancing at your watch, you can tell that the class must have started about twenty minutes ago. You walk quietly and quickly to your seat and hope Ms. Hawkins won't make much of it. To your surprise, no one seems to notice you. You take your seat and try to look as if nothing has happened.

You'd expect Liz Williams in the seat next to you to whisper something, or at least look at you—after all, you've been away quite a while.

"Hey, Liz, psst!"

No response. What's the matter with her? You poke her with your pencil. She doesn't budge.

It's as if you weren't even there!

"Does anyone know how many justices are on the Supreme Court of the United States?" Ms. Hawkins asks the class.

No one answers. You're the only one to raise your hand, but Ms. Hawkins doesn't notice. Neither does anyone else.

"Nine!" you call out. Still, no one notices.

"Well, the answer is nine," Ms. Hawkins says. "One chief justice and eight associate justices."

By this point you think you're losing your mind!

"Ms. Hawkins!" you shout. "Didn't you hear me? I said nine."

"Now, how do you suppose someone gets to be a Supreme Court justice?" Ms. Hawkins asks the class. No one answers, so she starts explaining how justices are selected.

"Ms. Hawkins!" you shout again. "Can you hear me? Wendy, Liz, Matt . . ."

Still no one notices. Could the Cave of Time have made you invisible?

Suddenly all eyes turn toward the classroom door.

"Well, look who's here!"

Ms. Hawkins, still looking at the doorway,

calls out your name. "Don't just stand there, take your seat, and after class I want to hear where you've been for the past few days!"

You blink your eyes and look again. There's still no one near the doorway. Glancing at your watch, you see it's been exactly three minutes since you came in.

Suddenly you realize what happened. It's what the oracle talked about. You're in another time frame, caught in two different perceptions of time. That's why the you that you think you are is invisible to everyone else: Your time frame is three minutes ahead of theirs. No one could see you until three minutes after you walked in, and when you spoke, no one could hear your voice until three minutes had passed. It's a horrible situation! You've got to get back to the Cave of Time!

You run out of the classroom, then stop at the doorway and look back.

Nobody noticed what you did. You realize that for the next three minutes, they will still see you sitting in your seat! You jog down the hallway and out of the school. Somehow you'll find your way to the Cave of Time. You'll stow away on a bus. At least you won't have to pay any fare—no one will notice you, at least not for the first three minutes!

You start to cross the street. There are no cars coming, but you have a frightening thought: You could be hit by a car because its driver won't be able to see you for three minutes. Should you take the risk of crossing?

Risk crossing the street to get to the bus station, turn to page 10.

Don't risk it, turn to page 20.

When you tell Yamara of your decision to remain in the present time, he steps forward and raises both hands, as if to salute you. You try not to shrink back from the ugly knobs on his head, thinking that if, in the future, everyone has knobs like that, they won't think they are ugly. Instead they will think that you're ugly because you *don't* have knobs on your head!

"You will not regret your decision," says Yamara.

"Henceforth you shall be an Earth Healer. Because you were born on Earth, you shall have your own cubicle in our underground city."

"What will I do as an Earth Healer?" you ask.

"You will be given a fleet of robot craft to maneuver from a central control station. You will guide them in their rehabilitation tasks. When you have completed two hundred years of service, you will be awarded a personal spacecraft, and you will be free to settle anywhere on Earth or in any of the colonies in the solar system."

"But two hundred years!" you interrupt. "I'll never live that long."

"You wouldn't have in your former time," Yamara replies, "but with our age-inhibiting treatment you should live at least three million years."

"Yamara," you say, "I think you've got a deal."

The End

You wait until the light turns red again and run into the path of a truck.

The End

You consider your three basic needs if you're to make it through the winter: food, warmth, and protection from predators. You study the Neanderthal shelter with new interest. About nine feet above the ground is a ledge, which can be reached by a series of handholds and footholds chipped into the wall. While the tribe was living here, the ledge was used as a sacred place. You weren't allowed to climb to it, but now your life may depend on the safety it offers. You grab a handhold and test it. You must be especially careful in everything you do. There's no one to take care of you if you're hurt.

Once you climb onto the ledge, your spirits rise. It's about twenty feet long and, though not wide, slants slightly inward, so you're not likely to roll off while sleeping.

Best of all, a spring trickles out of the wall near one end of the ledge. You'll be able to get fresh water without even coming down to the ground.

Now you have hope, and with it comes a surge of energy. A few animal skins were left by the Neanderthals, and you use them to make warm clothes and blankets. In the days that follow, you gather nuts and root vegetables and mend broken spears and sharpen knives so you can hunt and track small game.

Bundled in animal skins and sheltered from winter winds, you spend a lot of time sleeping. Sometimes you imagine that you are a hibernating bear.

The weeks wear on. You find nuts and berries, and even kill some small game, but you're not getting enough calories to maintain your weight. You tire easily. But you're determined not to give up. Even when you don't feel like stirring, you force yourself to hunt. You become better at it.

One day you hit a rabbit thirty feet away with a rock. You haven't learned to make a fire, so you have to eat raw meat. You don't like it, but eat it you must if you're to survive.

In time, you notice that the days are getting longer. Each day the sun rises higher in the sky. The snow is beginning to melt. One day, at dusk, you hear voices. The tribe has returned from their migration, bearing litters heaped with frozen reindeer meat! You run out to meet your old friends.

"Ug moogar wooam!" they keep saying.

You're not sure you understand the words,

but you can tell that they are amazed that you survived the winter. You are glad to see that Vor is not among them. You learn that he was trampled to death by a mammoth. It's a shock to hear this, but not something you'll shed tears about.

That night the chief comes up to you, smiling. *"Ug magwa win,"* he says.

Later you learn that the words mean "One day you will be chief."

The End

You bite into the first berry. Despite its strange flavor, tasting it makes you even hungrier. You eat another. You are about to swallow yet another when you begin to feel dizzy. You spit it out, but a moment later feel a sharp pain in your stomach. You try to walk, but your head is spinning—you're afraid you'll fall over. You take a step, then fall, doubled over in pain. It won't last long. You have only a minute to live.

The End

You pass up the berries and walk downstream along the riverbank, looking for food and a human settlement. If there's one nearby, you're likely to find it near the river.

Your instincts are right! You've gone a little more than half a mile when you smell smoke. Smoke . . . People . . . Cooking . . . Food! You quicken your pace, eager to find others, hoping they will welcome you.

A deep-throated growl sounds behind you. You whirl and see a striped animal charging right at you! Its long upper teeth are shaped to sink into flesh. There's no time to run, no tree to climb. You brace for the death that's sure to come.

Instead you hear a thump, then another. With a yelp the animal swerves. *Thump*. It rolls over, dying or dead. Three sharp rocks lie next to its body. Several pale-skinned humanlike creatures emerge from the woods. They are stockily built and have bony brows, like those of Iaark, the boy you met in the cave. From pictures you've seen, you know that they are probably Neanderthals, a subspecies of humans that coexisted with our ancestors for tens of thousands of years. They gather around you, talking in their strange tongue. You strain to catch the meaning of their

words. One of them smiles and touches your back.

The Neanderthals lead you to their camp, a hundred yards farther downriver. It is set in a flat, gravelly area protected by a huge overhanging rock. It would make a poor shelter against winter storms, you think, but it seems to be the only shelter they have. There are about twelve people in the camp, including a baby. Iaark is not among them.

"Iaark?" you ask.

No one replies. He's probably from another tribe.

Most of the people greet you with friendly curiosity. A woman gives you a stone bowl filled with ripe blueberries. You try them. They couldn't be better!

Continue to page 81.

In the days that follow, the Neanderthals treat you as one of them. They don't seem bothered by your different look. You doubt that you could ever master their language, but you learn from them how to hunt and fish and gather food. Only one of them makes you uneasy: a boy named Vor, who is about your age. He likes to come up and jab you with a stick and call you names you can't understand. The Neanderthals are generally a peaceable and easygoing people, and the adults don't seem to know what to make of Vor. When he jabs or taunts you, they turn their eyes the other way.

One day, while you and Vor are picking cloudberries on the cliffs that border the river, he jabs you so hard that you almost fall to your death. You turn on him, but he throws down his stick and stands, feet wide apart, ready to battle.

The Neanderthals are stronger than modern humans. You wouldn't have a chance fighting him, so you walk away and return to camp.

One evening soon afterward, the chief calls everyone around the fire and begins a long speech. You have trouble making out what he's saying, but the gist of it seems to be this: The reindeer are leaving—heading east on their annual migration. Food will soon be scarce, and the tribe must pack up and follow the herd.

One member of the tribe, a young man named Azog, has made a raft. He has decided to use it to journey down the river in search of better land. Two others—Larga and her daughter, Mi—have agreed to accompany him. Mi is a girl about your age whom you like very much.

The chief speaks of how he will miss Azog, Larga, and Mi, and he wishes them good luck.

He looks at you and says, *"Ug snn."*

You understand. You must decide whether to go with the tribe and follow the reindeer migration or join Azog, Larga, and Mi on a trip downriver to the land of the unknown.

Azog tells you that you are welcome to join them. He and Larga and Mi need to spend a day or two more in camp while they gather food and supplies. The rest of the tribe will be leaving in the morning.

That night you barely sleep, wondering what to do. The more you think about it, the more you want to be with your own people—modern humans. The Neanderthals are humans too, but a different subspecies. You're not sure you want to spend the rest of your life with them. Besides that, you know that the Neanderthals became extinct, whereas modern humans survived.

The chief himself wakes you in the morning. You understand what he is saying, even though you don't understand the exact words: You must make your decision.

Go with the tribe, turn to page 93.

Go with Azog, Larga, and Mi on the raft, turn to page 94.

Go off on your own and search for modern humans, turn to page 40.

Earth may not be like it was, but it's your home. You wonder how far into the future you've journeyed. A thousand years? A million years?

A screen lights up. You're determined to see what happened to Earth, so you order the computer to stay on course. Moments later, retro-rockets fire to brake the descent.

INSTRUCTIONS FOR SURVIVAL ON EARTH

Oxygen content: 4.3 percent.
Supplementary oxygen-generating
helmet must be worn at all times.
Radioactivity level: 6. Radiation-resistant
coat and helmet cover must be worn
except in protected zones. Basic gene
grain bits are available. This is the only
edible food. Ingest 1,800 milligrams of
vitragranules anti-toxicant formula mark
8744369-5 with each kilogram of gene
grain bits. All water must be demulsified
and deacidified in puroscan.

You have hardly finished reading these words when you feel an abrupt deceleration followed by a slight jolt. Your craft has made an amazingly smooth landing.

Through the window you see an endless landscape of rocks and boulders, the sort you might find in a dried-up riverbed. So this is Earth.

You only hope it's not all like this.

You put on the oxygen-generating helmet and your radiation-resistant coat and helmet cover, open the hatch, and step outside. Your computer said that food is available, but everywhere you look, you see nothing but barren, rust-colored rocks and dirt. It's the most forlorn landscape you've ever seen.

There's no way of knowing which way to walk.

Before you can think about it, a strange-looking machine zooms in and hovers over you. You watch with fascination as wire arms descend, and you realize that they are about to enfold your spacecraft like a spider capturing a fly.

Jump back into your spacecraft, turn to page 105.

Stay where you are and watch what happens, turn to page 58.

You walk up the slope toward the rocky ridge. You've taken about a dozen steps when the rainbow disappears. The clouds grow thicker, the wind blows harder. You feel like the last reserves of energy are draining from your body, but you force yourself to keep climbing, step by step.

The wind blows in violent gusts. You hunch over, trying to keep the chill from taking over your body. Finally, you approach the top of the ridge. What lies behind it? Something must, because you smell smoke!

The thought that people may be nearby gives you renewed energy. A few steps more and you reach a ledge from which you can look down on the valley ahead of you. The smoke is coming from a niche in the side of a cliff. You work your way around to it. Someone has built a fire in the mouth of the cave. A woman is adding sticks to the fire. You hurry toward her.

The woman sees you and calls the others. Half a dozen people come out to greet you. You see at once that these are modern humans, not Neanderthals. You can't understand their language, but you can tell that they are happy

to see you. Two or three of them are about your age.

It takes a dinner of herb soup, dried mammoth meat, and berries while sitting in front of a hot fire before you finally warm up. Before you go to bed, the woman you first met carries a torch and takes you deeper into the cave to show you paintings on the wall of antelopes, deer, hawks, and other creatures. You're amazed at how expressive and realistic they are.

She leads you to a far corner of the cave and points to a tunnel entrance. Using gestures, she lets you know that you should never enter it, that someone did once and never came back.

Spring has come. You've been living with the cave people for six months now and have learned many new skills. You're amazed by how cooperative and friendly everyone is. This is the way people should be, you think.

A few days ago you crawled a little ways into the tunnel the woman showed you, wondering if it might lead to the Cave of Time. You've enjoyed living with the cave people and have made some good friends, but someday you may want the excitement of going to a different time. Meanwhile, you're happy where you are.

The End

If, after a while, you get tired of living with the cave people and decide to explore the tunnel, turn to page 49.

You ask the computer to redirect you to Sintra. G-forces almost crush you as your spacecraft accelerates. It's as if you suddenly weigh three hundred pounds—the price of rapid travel through space!

More than an hour passes before your craft stops accelerating and you resume your former weightlessness. You are now coasting—at what tremendous speed you have no idea.

As you are relaxing, a buzzer sounds and words appear on your video screen:

> Stand by for hibernation treatment. When you come out of hibernation 83.5 Earth years from now, you will find yourself on the planet Sintra of Number 8,773,389—a highly stable, class G star. Sintra is one of the most beautiful, abundant, habitable planets in the galaxy. Conditions are almost identical to those that existed on Earth during the early days of humans on that planet.

You try to imagine what life will be like on Sintra, but you're soon asleep.

• • •

Your next sensation is of a dull electric shock in your head, then another, and another. You flail your arms, as if trying to brush away a fly. You want to go back to sleep. But there's no chance of that! The mild shocks persist for a few moments. Then loud music is playing in your ears. When it stops, a voice speaks:

> "You are awakening from hibernation.
> Your spacecraft has landed on Sintra.
> Atmosphere and temperature are well
> suited for human life. You may open the
> hatch whenever you want."

Your mind is flooded with questions. *What's this planet like? What sort of people live here? What kinds of animals and plants are there? How advanced is their technology?* You can't wait to see!

You stretch, sit up, and look out the window. On one side is a cluster of brightly painted houses; on the other a beautiful park rimmed by giant ferns. In the center is a splendid fountain. You throw open the hatch and breathe the fresh, clean air. At the same time several large tear-shaped saucer cars silently approach your capsule and land nearby. Smiling and holding out bouquets of flowers, the inhabitants of Sintra greet you.

The End

The tribe spends the morning preparing for the journey. Packing up everything—fur skins for extra warmth during the cold months ahead, flint for starting fires, bags of extra food (nuts, dried fruit, and edible roots), spices and oils for making medicines, spears for bringing down game, and crude stone knives—takes all day. But early the following morning, after a breakfast of river crabs and onion roots, you and the Neanderthals begin the long trek.

About noon you reach a place where a swiftly running river is shallow enough to ford. The chief leads the way, stepping cautiously from rock to rock. The rest of the tribe follows single file. You are last in line. Stepping carefully across the rocks, you concentrate on your balance. If you fall, the strong current would sweep you downstream so fast you'd never get back. As you approach the trickiest section of the crossing, you notice that Vor has dropped back in line and is now the next person ahead of you. He could easily jab you and knock you into the river. Why else would he want to get so close to you? Maybe you should turn around and try to join Azog, Larga, and Mi. They said that they wouldn't leave for another day.

Take your chances with Vor, turn to page 110.
Go back to camp, turn to page 60.

The next morning the rest of the tribe leaves in pursuit of the reindeer. Only you, Azog, Larga, and Mi are left. The four of you gather food and decide what you can bring.

The following morning you take a close look at the raft. It's not much more than a few dozen logs lined up side by side and bound loosely with vines. If you run into a rough stretch of rapids, it will almost certainly come apart. Thinking about it, you realize that the Neanderthals aren't very smart at certain things. Or maybe the problem is that it wasn't smart of you to think they could build a sturdy raft.

It's too late to change your mind now. Azog pushes off, and the four of you start down the river. Instead of paddles you have long poles you use to steer the raft by thrusting one end against the river bottom.

Each afternoon you camp on a grassy bank. Azog and Larga work patiently to catch trout in their crude nets. Mi gathers fruit and nuts. You do your best to tighten the vines that hold the raft together, and you add new vines for extra strength.

All goes well for the first few days. You grow to like Mi a lot. People living in modern times might say that she's ugly because of her bony forehead, but when she smiles, she looks so happy that you begin to think that Neanderthals look just as good as modern people.

After your work is done, you and Mi play together. She is stronger than you but not as well coordinated. Though she can break branches that you can hardly bend, you throw stones straighter and truer than she can.

One day you reach a stretch where the river is too deep to pole the raft. That doesn't bother any of you—you can just drift with the current. You stretch out and listen to Larga telling stories about the tribe she came from. She's telling one of her tales when you hear a rushing noise up ahead. At first you think it's the wind, then you think it's rapids, then you realize it's a waterfall!

Using words you've learned, you shout, *"Vg wamp!"*—"We must get to the shore!" You start paddling with your pole. The others sit motionless, staring at you. *Why aren't they paddling?*

Stunned, you realize that they have never heard the sound of a waterfall; they have never even heard of a waterfall! The loud noise ahead doesn't mean any more to them than would the roar of a jet plane.

The raft is drifting faster now. The noise of the falls becomes a roar. You have to shout to be heard. At last the Neanderthals understand the danger. They do not yell or cry out. Instead, each of them pats your shoulder, as if to say good-bye. Seconds later your raft hurtles over the falls.

In the long fraction of time that you are falling, you see the river ahead of you winding downstream, looking strangely narrowed, as if most of the water is flowing into the ground. Then the raft breaks apart, and you are thrown into the torrent. The force of it almost wrenches your body in two as it sweeps you into the darkness beneath the surface. You feel Mi brush against you as she slides by.

You're sure you're going to drown, but strangely the water thins: You can breathe, and you feel a thrill of hope because you have a strong feeling that you have entered the Cave of Time! There's a chance you are going to survive! With luck, your Neanderthal friends will survive too, which is your last thought before you fall unconscious.

Continue to page 97.

You awaken in darkness. You sense that you have entered a new time and that you are in a strange place in this new time. The ground you're on seems to be moving under your feet. For a moment you can see nothing, but you hear noises—people groaning, murmuring. They sound as if they are in pain, but you cannot see them.

You take small steps.

The motion you feel throws you off balance, sending you headlong over a body and onto a wooden surface. At that moment you realize where you are!

Dark-skinned men and women are chained to the walls and floor of this dank gloomy space. A few thin bands of light seep through cracks of the roof. You guess that you are on a ship and that the sun has come out and is shining onto the deck above you. You also realize that this is no ordinary ship. It is a slave ship, probably heading for America.

You are saddened by the sight of the faces around you. They look so broken, so tired. You have learned in school about the slave trade in Africa, the Caribbean Islands, and the American colonies, but what you see now is

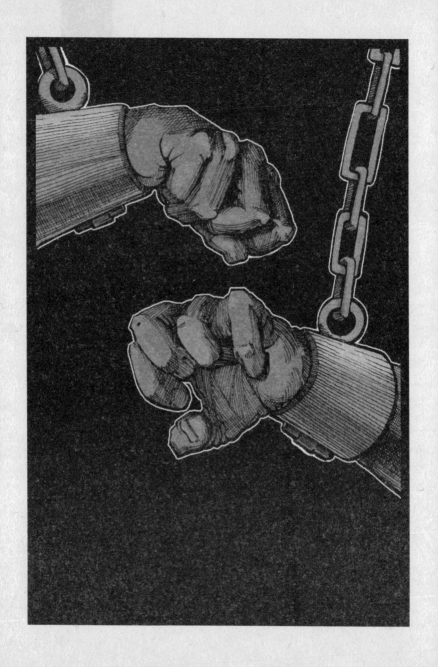

beyond words. Piled one on top of another, like produce in a carton, are people dehumanized, stripped of their pride and dignity.

Try to set the people free, turn to page 54.

Climb up on deck and look for the captain, turn to page 62.

You wake up in a tiny spacecraft. You're in a chair molded to your body. Stars are visible in all directions. To your left and slightly behind you is Saturn, with its spectacular rings. To your right is Jupiter. Its famous red spot has broken into three flecks of orange, but its four largest moons are as prominent as they were to Galileo when he discovered them long before you were born.

Directly ahead is a red-hued planet—Mars. You must be close to it, because it looks brighter and larger even though its diameter is twenty times smaller than Saturn.

Beyond Mars is another planet. The large moon near it tells you that it must be Earth, but it doesn't look like the Earth you remember, with the swirls of white clouds over blue oceans and brown-and-green-hued land mass. The entire planet is covered with thick gray clouds!

Has the sun stopped shining on Earth? Is its total cloud cover the result of the greenhouse effect, caused by the increase of carbon dioxide in the air? Scientists warned that this might happen back in your own time.

Could you stand to live on such a planet? It's a horrible prospect, but where else can you go? Mars, perhaps. Maybe there's a colony there, and

Mars is quite close by. You look at the instrument panel and control levers. It may take a while to learn how to steer this craft, but the computer will take care of the hard part. Why not take control and head toward Mars? If you see signs of a colony, you could land.

Take control and head to Mars, turn to page 103.

Let your spacecraft continue on to Earth,
turn to page 102.

Your trip to Earth goes well; your craft smoothly brakes as it approaches Earth's atmosphere. Suddenly you can't see anything through your windows but the dense clouds that cover the planet.

A voice comes from speakers on the instrument panel.

"Greetings from Earth Orbit Monitor Twenty-Two-Two-Two. We have been advised by Suprema Eighty-Seven to the Fifth Power that you wish to land. Normally, only archaeologists and reconstructionists visit Earth. It is not classified as a habitable planet. Nearly all descendants of Earth's survivors have moved to distant colonies. Are you sure you want to land? If not, we can redirect you to Sintra, which has an environment similar to the one Earth had during its prime eons."

Decide to land on Earth anyway, turn to page 84.
Ask to be redirected to Sintra, turn to page 90.

When you pull on a lever, a hologram appears, showing objects for hundreds of millions of miles around you. Accompanying it are readouts of distances and bearings. You touch another lever. A green arrow on the hologram points toward Earth. Using the lever and turning the arrow slightly, you're able to point it toward Mars.

You feel the spacecraft turning, then steadying on a new course.

A red arrow flashes, pointed toward a small object, undoubtedly an asteroid. It's about one hundred thousand miles away, then seventy thousand, then forty thousand. . . . Your spacecraft turns very slightly to avoid the asteroid, then turns again until you're back on course to Mars.

Mars grows larger and larger ahead of you until it fills half the holographic screen. You're close enough now to see surface features like mountains and canyons. It's time to get the spacecraft to brake and go into Martian orbit so you can look for a place to land.

You work the other levers, experimenting. You're thrown back in your seat as the spacecraft suddenly accelerates. You're hurtling toward Mars at terrifying speed. Now, instead of cruising through space, you're diving toward the surface.

You pull on a lever you hadn't tried before. A red light comes on. A buzzer sounds. You pull on two levers at a time. The craft brakes. The spacecraft is slowing. You didn't realize how low it was, headed toward a Martian mountain, in fact right into it!

The End

You jump back into the spacecraft and shut the hatch—just in time, because within seconds it lifts off so fast you're almost knocked out by the g-force. Your computer must have sensed that you were being attacked and applied full thrust the moment you were aboard.

The ground passes by at tremendous speed as you traverse the landscape. You watch in mixed fascination and horror at the terrain passing by below: gouged hills and desolate valleys blanketed by stones, weeds, vines, and occasional ruins of cities. You cross a dried-up riverbed and pass over gutted skyscrapers, buildings toppled into rusting shards of steel beams. You feel heartsick witnessing the horrible things that have happened since you left your own time.

Your spacecraft passes over a barren hillside. Beyond it is a huge silver dome. The craft slows and maneuvers toward it. A panel slides open, and you enter—into total darkness. You sense that the spacecraft is gently settling down.

Motion stops. You're on the ground. The hatch slides open. Lights come on. You are in an enormous hangar. Three small tear-shaped cars careen around a corner and abruptly stop. Humanlike creatures emerge from them. They

are dressed in identical brown robes. You could mistake them for people from your own time except for the knobs growing out of their heads.

One of them steps toward you. He speaks in English, but in an odd artificial tone. You wonder if he is an android.

"Welcome to Earth," he says. "I am Yamara, Consul of Solar Seven. We were notified that you were coming and that you were born on Earth and traveled through a time warp."

"Through the Cave of Time," you say.

"It is the same thing."

"You've heard about it?"

"There is a legend."

"Where are we on Earth?" you ask.

"In Golor, on the continent of America."

He pulls out a small device and touches the screen, which immediately expands to about two square feet in size. A map appears. It's a map of Earth, but one that looks very different from the Earth you know. Australia has merged with Asia. Antarctica has drifted almost to Hawaii. North and South America have become one big blob. You realize that you must have been transported millions of years into the future.

"Since you were born on Earth, you may stay here," says Yamara.

"Where will I live? What will I do?" you ask.

"You will become one of us," says Yamara. "We are Earth Healers, charged by the planetary council to supervise Earth's recovery. We have already improved its environment tenfold. We are proud of our work healing the Earth."

"From what I've seen, there's not much to be proud of," you say. "No sunshine, no grass or flowers; only a few sickly looking weeds, cities in ruins—"

Your host interrupts. "Do not judge us, the living, for the terrible things that happened in Earth's history. Our robot craft spend twenty-four hours a day cleaning up debris and neutralizing radioactive sources. In some areas of the world the sun shines through, often for five or ten minutes, or even longer, and trees and plants are growing. Each century carbon monoxide and other toxins decrease. Oxygen increases. Now you can sometimes take off your helmet and breathe the air for a few minutes. In a few million years Earth will be filled with plant and animal life, and the oceans and rivers and lakes and air will be as clear and pure as they were before humans spread over the planet."

You are moved by the noble goals of the Earth Healers. "This world, which for me is the world of the future, is very interesting," you say, "but I want to return to my own time. Did you say there's a legend about the Cave of Time?"

"Yes, the cave that legends tell of is some five hundred kilometers distant. I could take you there, but you should know this: Many people have entered the cave, but none have come out. Animals sometimes come out. Their bones lie scattered near the entrance because they have no oxygen helmets and cannot survive for more than a few hours."

You listen eagerly to what Yamara says. If the place he speaks of is the Cave of Time, there's a chance you could return to your own time. The only trouble is that you might end up at a time that's worse than the one you're in.

Seek out the Cave of Time, turn to page 65.
Stay in the time you're in now, turn to page 71.

You step cautiously onto the next rock. Vor is waiting for you just ahead. You leap from the last rock to the big one where he's standing. He raises a thick stick and jabs it toward your gut. You ward it off, lose your balance, and fall into the water. For a moment you can touch bottom with one foot, but the current sweeps you into deeper water. Your enemy is no longer Vor—it's the raging river!

You remember not to panic. In the swirling choppy water your head is bound to be under-water part of the time. Using the breaststroke and frog kick to get the power you need, you're able to get up to the surface often enough to breathe. You're making progress toward shore when a wave hits just as you take a breath. You cough and sputter. The current sweeps you into a rock, which bruises your shoulder. One of your feet touches bottom, but again the current sweeps you away. You keep fighting the waves, stroking steadily. Minutes later you manage to make it to the shore, pull yourself up onto a large flat rock, lie back, and close your eyes. When you open them, the Neanderthals are gathered around you.

"*Ug mroosuma,*" the chief says as you sit up.

Vor is standing in the back of the group, his head bowed. It is obvious that everyone is impressed that you survived your ordeal. Although the Neanderthals are stronger than modern humans, they are poor swimmers, and none of them could have done what you did.

The chief puts an arm around you. *"Ug soma voorum,"* he says. He points to the sky, then to you. The other Neanderthals nod in agreement.

As usual, you can't understand the exact words, but you can guess the meaning: The chief believes that you have magical powers and has chosen you to be the shaman—the wise person of the tribe. You need not fear Vor any longer, and you don't think it will be hard to meet the chief's expectations. After all, you're planning to invent the wheel.

The End

Late that evening you squirm your way through the porthole and drop onto the deck. Because the ship is anchored, only one man is on watch. You see him standing on the afterdeck, gazing at the moon. Keeping low, you work your way up to the bow. The water looks black, except for the patches of reflected moonlight. You climb over the side, grab hold of the anchor chain, slide down, and drop noiselessly into the sea. With strong, firm strokes you start swimming toward the shore.

A flash of light startles you. It's just a patch of phosphorous, but it makes you think of other perils. With each stroke you wonder whether a shark or stingray will attack.

It's not long before you feel yourself tiring. Looking back, you see the *Bounty* riding peacefully at anchor. Land seems no closer than when you started out. For a moment you think of trying to make it back to the ship.

But then you realize that the current has been carrying you away from the ship and along the coast. You remember to relax and stroke steadily through the water—that helps. You feel calmer. Maybe you'll make it. Still, you know that your strength is ebbing. You begin to think you won't make it.

You are thinking this when you hear a sound ahead, a rhythmic *slap, slap, slap* of the waves on a tiny island, no more than a strand of black coral jutting out of the sea.

You swim with renewed energy. In a few minutes you touch bottom. A wave carries you up onto a flat area. You get a grip on the coral, the wave recedes, and you pull yourself onto dry land. You flop exhausted on the coral beach and quickly fall asleep.

Hours later the morning sun awakens you. You are still about half a mile from the main island of Tahiti, but there are a few small boats nearby. At the far end of your tiny reef a boy is wading through the shallow water, looking for crabs. You notice each other at the same time. He pulls his canoe onto the reef and calls to you. You walk to meet him.

"Mowli," he says, pointing to himself.

You point to yourself and say your name. Then you point to the *Bounty*, then again to yourself, and make motions, as if you were swimming. Then you point to yourself, then to the *Bounty*, and move your hand under your chin, as if someone were slitting your throat.

Mowli understands. He motions you to follow

him and leads you back to his canoe. You spend the next hour helping him catch crabs. When the sun is so high you're afraid it will burn off the tops of your ears, Mowli paddles you ashore and takes you home to his thatched hut. There, you meet his parents, his sister, and their goats, chickens, and dog. Almost at once you feel like you're one of the family.

A few days later, standing on a bluff overlooking the sea, you watch the *Bounty* weigh anchor and set sail. You never find out whether Fletcher Christian and his crew of mutineers found a safe island or whether they were captured and hung by the British, though you do learn that Captain Bligh and most of his loyal crew survived their perilous voyage in the *Bounty*'s longboat.

As for you, though you miss your family and friends very much, you could hardly enjoy life more than on the beautiful island of Tahiti, where work is like play, strangers become friends, coconuts are free for the taking, and you can sail and swim until you are so tired that the minute you lie down each night, you're floating in a happy dream.

The End

You run out of the cave, hoping the bear won't follow. The terrain around you is studded with boulders. You hide behind the nearest one and peer around the edge. The bear is standing at the entrance of the cave, rearing up, sniffing the air. You hope it won't catch your scent.

After a few minutes the bear turns around and goes back into the cave. You think about the boy, Iaark, and wonder where he went. He looked like he could take care of himself.

Ahead of you are grasslands that slope steeply toward a river far below. You hurry down the slope, weaving among the great boulders, then through meadowlands. At last you reach the river. Standing by the swift-flowing water, you feel the terror of being alone. You are lost, not merely in the wilderness, but in a time in the past, when "civilization"—if you ever find it—will be nothing more than a tribe of cave people.

You look around nervously, thinking that at any moment a bear or some other carnivore—maybe one that doesn't exist in your own time—will attack. You notice a patch of brush with yellow leaves and red berries. You realize that you're hungry. You can't be sure those berries aren't poisonous, but you'll have to take some chances, you think. Otherwise you'll starve to death.

Eat some red berries, turn to page 77.

Pass up the berries, turn to page 78.

You leap high against the cave wall, grab a handhold, dig the toe of your right foot into a tiny niche, and begin to climb. Looking over your shoulder, you see the bear lumbering toward you, grunting and snorting.

You're able to climb a few feet higher, but the wall becomes even steeper above you. Your feet are still within the bear's reach, and you can't find a higher handhold! Suddenly your wrist is seized in a tight grip, and you feel yourself rising, then being hauled onto a ledge. Only then does the grip release you. Aching and sore, you look into the smiling eyes of Iaark, then back at the claws of the bear raking the lip of the ledge, trying to reach you.

"*Aug*," says Iaark. He starts crawling ahead into a dark tunnel.

You wonder whether to follow him. He saved your life, so you're pretty sure you can trust him, but you don't know anything about him except that he's tremendously strong.

Follow Iaark, turn to page 120.
Wait until the bear is gone and then get out of the cave,
turn to page 122.

You follow Iaark into the tunnel, hoping it will come out in the open. "Where does this lead?" you ask, though you know he can't understand your language.

"*Orgorjon,*" he calls back.

You have no idea what that means, but the tone of it was friendly. Maybe he's just exploring the tunnel to see where it goes.

Iaark continues on. You follow close behind, thinking that you may come out on the other side of the mountain. Instead, the tunnel floor gives way. You're falling, and Iaark is falling with you, tumbling through the Cave of Time! Then you are waking, as if from a dream. Once again you're just inside the entrance of a cave. You walk out into the open air. Something—maybe it's the smell of grass and flowers or the temperature or the sound of traffic from a nearby highway—tells you that you're back in your own time!

"*Ak lugga!*" says a voice. It's Iaark, walking toward you from the interior of the cave.

"Iaark, you're here—I can't believe it! You'd better come with me," you call. "You're going to need a place to stay."

The two of you reach a road and walk along it to a nearby town. Iaark gasps at the sight of cars and trucks going by on the highway. Your time is stranger to him than his time was to you!

When you reach the town and talk to a police officer standing on a street corner, you find that you are indeed back in your own time, and you'll be taking a Neanderthal boy home with you!

The End

After a while the bear shuffles off.

I'd better get out of here before it comes back, you think. You take a last look around the cave. Your eyes rest on a niche in the wall that you hadn't noticed before. You walk over to inspect it more closely. It's the entrance to another tunnel. Should you follow it?

Explore the tunnel, continue to page 123.

Get out of the cave while you have the chance, turn to page 116.

To your surprise, the tunnel only winds around for a hundred yards or so before it comes out into the open air. The entrance is almost blocked by vines and shrubs, but you make your way through them.

You've come out on the other side of the mountain—at least that's where you guess you are. You're not sure if you're still in the same time. You start down the mountain and soon reach a forest of giant pines.

You're thirsty. There's no sign of water. You know that if you keep going down the mountain, you're likely to reach a river or stream. You enter the forest and work your way down the slope.

Resting a moment, you hear a familiar sound: running water. You hurry on and come to a stream. A man and a woman, dressed in animal skins, are trying to spear fish with pointed sticks. You watch quietly for a moment. You're close enough to see that they are not Neanderthals. They're modern humans, like you. You step forward and call out, "Hello there!"

They look around, smiling.

"Haru wama," the woman calls.

"*Hara wu,*" the man says.

By the looks on their faces you know you've made friends.

The End

You say "Pequod," but nothing happens.

For the rest of your life Pitcairn Island will be your home.

The End

You spend several days preparing for your journey.

Mornings you gather nuts and edible roots. Afternoons you sew animal hides using a bone splinter for a needle and pig gut for thread. You cut and tie a triple layer of deerskins together to serve as boots, and spend long hours making a warm coat.

Finally, you fashion a backpack out of a bearskin and vines. You're in excellent physical condition—you can move at a good pace.

The morning you plan to leave dawns cold and clear, with a dusting of snow on the ground. Using the sun as your compass, you head south, cutting through stretches of pine forest and rocky highlands. Shortly after midday you hear the howling of a wolf, then another, and another. You quicken your step, hoping to find a shelter of some sort—a niche in the rocks or a tree with branches low enough to climb— but you feel a deepening sense of fear. No natural shelter can save you for long, and there is no chance of finding a house, cabin, or road, because there are none now—tens of thousands of years in the past.

The wolves sound closer now. They must

have picked up your scent. You see one, then another. They edge closer. Yet another wolf joins them, then two more; five now, great gray creatures with fanged jaws. You try not to make eye contact, because you've heard that predators take this to mean a challenge. You know you shouldn't run. If you did, the wolves would think of you as prey. You slowly back away, trying to give yourself time to think.

For the moment the wolves seem content to stand and watch you, but you know that at any moment they may move in for the kill. You are still trying to think if there's anything you can do when you hear a deep throaty growl behind you. You whirl around and look up at the most frightening sight of your life: a saber-toothed tiger sitting on a high boulder not more than forty feet away. You have a feeling that if it weren't for the tiger, the wolves would have already attacked!

Now the wolves begin to advance on you, but very cautiously. They are obviously wary of the tiger, which could be on top of them in a couple of bounds. It's not much consolation that the wolves are scared of the tiger. You're scared of all of them!

The wolves have their eyes on the tiger, but they take another step toward you, then another. Again the tiger growls. What should you do?

Play dead and hope that the tiger and the wolves won't go after you, continue to page 131.

Stay alert and be ready to act depending on what happens, turn to page 142.

Step sideways, so you won't be between the tiger and the wolves, turn to page 150.

You flop on the ground, planning to play dead, hoping the wolves will pay attention to the tiger, which is crouched on its boulder looking down on all of you. All but one wolf does, but that one has kept its eyes on you. Now it begins to move closer. If you play dead, it's not going to be fooled, and you'll have no chance of defending yourself. You get to your feet.

Walk toward the boulder the tiger is crouched on, turn to page 132.

Stand tall and talk loudly, turn to page 133.

You walk toward the boulder the tiger is crouched on. It's so surprised to see a creature your size coming toward it that it gets to its feet and blinks. You slow your pace. The wolves are surprised too, and hang back. That's a relief, but you're still in plenty of trouble.

Walk sideways, distancing yourself from both the tiger and the wolves, turn to page 134.

Try to reach a sharp rock that you notice, turn to page 135.

You stand as tall as you can and talk loudly. The wolves look at you curiously. None of them attack, but you know this won't last long. You've got to think of something better!

Walk off to the side, hoping to get away from the area,
turn to page 139.

Look for a rock or stick you could grab,
turn to page 140.

You sidestep, leaving the tiger and wolves to confront one another.

You wish that's what would happen, but the tiger has gotten over its surprise and starts toward you, its jaws open, its saber teeth poised to pierce deep into your flesh.

You have seconds to live, no time to think.

The End

Four steps take you to the sharp rock you spotted. It's heavy to hold, but the added weight makes it a more formidable weapon.

You hold it in both hands, sharp end pointed forward, and look around.

The tiger leaps down from its perch. It walks cautiously toward you, but its eyes seem to be on the wolves.

Duck aside and hope the tiger goes after the wolves, turn to page 136.

Wait until it's close enough and try to bring your rock down on the tiger's jaws, turn to page 137.

You duck to one side. The tiger comes at you. You still have your rock, but the tiger could brush it aside with one swat of a paw.

It charges! You bring your rock down toward its nose, but the tiger twists to one side, and you're only able to strike a glancing blow before it sinks its teeth into your shoulder and flips you to the ground. You throw up your free arm to defend yourself, your last act before you die.

The End

You raise the rock. The tiger charges. You bring the sharp end down, cracking one of its saber teeth. You're thrown off balance and down for a moment, but instantly you're on your feet. The tiger lopes off, yowling in pain.

Now you have the wolves to deal with. For the moment they look confused, as if not able to understand how you conquered a tiger.

Head for the woods while the wolves are still confused,
turn to page 138.

Climb on the boulder the tiger was perched on,
turn to page 141.

The wolves are still sniffing around the spot where the tiger disappeared into the woods. If you run, it could attract their attention, so you walk sideways until you're out of sight, then break into a jog and head for the river, hoping the wolves forgot about you.

They didn't. You've gone only a short distance when you hear them coming. You start to look for a tree or a rock ledge where you could be safe, but in seconds they're on you. Your last thought is about how odd it is to die thousands of years before you were born.

The End

You walk off to the side, hoping the tiger and the wolves will fight it out. You've gone about forty feet when spiked teeth rip into your leg. You let out a scream, not sure whether it's a wolf or the tiger that's got you. Not that it matters.

The End

You see a couple of rocks that might be good. One is a heavy one. You would be able to lift it over your head, but it would be hard to swing it fast. A small, sharp-pointed rock nearby would be easier to swing, but it's too far away to reach in time—the wolves are coming at you. . . .

You pick up the heavy rock and hold it above your head. The first wolf comes at you. You bring the rock down, aiming for its muzzle. The wolf ducks to the side, and the rock grazes its shoulder. The wolf yelps in pain, but by the time you bring the rock up again, the others are on you.

One grips your ankle and twists you to the ground. Another clamps its jaws on your throat. You feel the blood gushing out for a second.

The End

You scramble up on the boulder where the tiger was perched. Judging by your last look at it— yowling off into the forest—you don't think it will be back soon.

You're still catching your breath when the wolves regroup at the base of the boulder. They leap up as high as they can, but don't have a chance of reaching you.

After a while the wolves give up and go off, looking for other game. You wait an hour more, giving them plenty of time to move on, then climb down from your perch. You're extremely tired and soon fall asleep.

When you wake up, the tiger is standing over you. You broke its biggest tooth, but it has plenty of others.

The End

Your only hope may be for the tigers and wolves to forget about you and fight one another, so for the moment you stand motionless, keeping alert. To your surprise, a wolf walks up to you, but instead of attacking, sniffs your feet. You have no idea what it's going to do next. You could try to twist into a better position, then kick it in the underbelly. That might send it off.

Twist so you can kick at the wolf, turn to page 144.
Don't move, but talk softly to it, continue to page 143.

You talk softly to the wolf. It gives a low throaty growl, but doesn't bite, so you keep talking. Very gently, you slide your hand along its neck. It starts—you're afraid it's going to bite—but it seems to understand you mean no harm as you rub its neck.

Meanwhile, you are watching the tiger and the other four wolves. The tiger leaps down from its perch and lopes off into the woods.

The other wolves chase it, but the wolf you've been petting stays by your side.

The other wolves may come back. It's not likely they will try to fight a tiger. You'd better get to the river, where they'd lose your scent.

"Come on, boy," you say to the wolf, and to your amazement, it trots along beside you.

You don't know it, but you have just acquired the world's first dog!

The End

You twist your body and aim a swift kick at the wolf's underbelly. The wolf yelps and limps off.

The other wolves are growling at the tiger, which is watching them from a distance. The wolf you kicked seems badly hurt. The other wolves look over at you, forget about the tiger, and charge you.

You outfought one wolf, but you can't out-fight four.

The End

I may freeze or starve without my backpack, but I won't live that long if I don't cover some distance, you think. You slip off your pack and run into the woods.

You've gone a few hundred yards when you notice a spruce tree with branches low enough for you to climb. Maybe you should climb it and wait until you're sure the tiger or wolves aren't chasing you. Then you could return and get your backpack.

Climb the tree and wait, turn to page 147.
Try to loop around to get to the river, turn to page 148.

You've got to keep your backpack—you'll freeze or starve without it, you think. You run into the woods, hoping to find a tree with branches low enough to climb or get down to the river so you can throw pursuing predators off the scent.

It's a good idea, except that you're out of breath after running a few hundred paces with your pack. The wolves were late getting started, but it takes only a minute for them to pick up your scent and run you down.

The End

You climb the tree, making sure you get high enough so the tiger can't reach you. Then you wait, afraid that predators might come by.

By the time a couple of hours have passed, you are stiff, cold, and hungry. You haven't seen or heard the wolves or the tiger. You can't spend the night up here. You've got to come down and get your backpack.

You let yourself down to the ground and head toward where you left your pack, trying to make as little noise as possible. You're confused as to the direction and waste an hour wandering around before you find the spot where you threw it down.

You wish you hadn't bothered to look. The wolves have eaten your food, torn your clothes to shreds, and defecated on what was left.

A chill wind has come up. The night is an exceptionally cold one. Without the clothes that were in your backpack, it's impossible to stay warm.

Vultures find your body, cold and still, in the morning.

At least you weren't eaten alive.

The End

You circle the tree once, hoping to confuse the wolves if they've followed your scent. Then you jog on at a fast pace, heading for the river.

Meanwhile, you try to think of a way to survive the night with no food and no warm clothes to protect yourself against the cold.

After about half an hour you break out of the woods and onto open land. It looks familiar. The mountainside ahead of you reminds you of the terrain near the Cave of Time. You could explore farther and hope to find the cave, but you're afraid it will get dark before you are able to find it.

You know that if you follow the slope downhill, you'll reach the river. That would supply drinking water, and maybe you'll find crayfish and watercress along the shore. Maybe you'll find people!

Climb up the slope in search of the Cave of Time, turn to page 151.

Head for the river, continue to page 149.

You head down the slope, thinking your chances will be better if you get to the river. By the time you get there, darkness is setting in. You're tremendously thirsty and gulp handfuls of cool water. You walk along the riverbank, turning over rocks, looking for crayfish. You've just found one when you smell smoke. There must be people up ahead! Clutching the crayfish in one hand, you hurry on. Soon you hear voices. Seconds later you come upon a tent crudely fashioned out of animal skins.

"Hello!" you call.

A girl comes out of the tent. It's Mi! Azog and Larga are right behind her! They run forward and happily greet you. You soon learn that they had to interrupt their raft trip because the vines that held the logs together had come loose. They feed you and provide you with animal skins to keep you warm during the night. The next morning you show them how to tie the logs so they won't come apart, and the four of you set out on the raft, headed downstream.

So it is that you are fated to live with a small group of Neanderthals. Their species will become extinct long before you were born, but not for several thousand years.

The End

You cautiously step to the side.

The wolves move closer to the tiger.

The tiger growls.

Suddenly one wolf comes at you. You look for a stick or rock to defend yourself, but see nothing. The wolf is only a few feet from you when the tiger pounces on it, knocks it to the ground, and rips open half its side.

The other four wolves are growling at the tiger. None of them are looking at you. This could be your chance to get away. Should you slip off your pack of extra clothes and food so as not to be weighed down?

Drop your pack and run for it, turn to page 145.

Keep your pack and run for it, turn to page 146.

You climb the slope, trying to move as fast as you can without exhausting yourself. The terrain above looks increasingly familiar. You reach a ridge from which a mountaintop is visible. Looking down, you can see the river. Now you know exactly where you are, which is lucky, for a cold wind has come up and the sun has dropped below the ridge to the west.

You quicken your pace. You're determined to find your way back to the Cave of Time. You walk along the river, looking for landmarks you remember. You're hungry and cold. After a half day's trek, you reach the bottom of a slope that extends down from a mountain.

The area looks familiar. You climb up the slope, winding around the boulders, stopping occasionally to rest and get your bearings. You reach an entrance to the cave shortly before sunset.

You enter it with care, peering as far inside as you can with each step. In the dim light you see a tunnel. It's not familiar, but you have a strong feeling that it will lead you to another time.

You explore to see how far it goes, groping with your hands ahead of you. The tunnel begins to slope down. You take another step and feel nothing underfoot. Then you're falling, sliding down a rock chute. You manage to break your descent with your feet and reach the bottom, shaken but with no broken bones.

Turn to page 57.